GRACE
STREET
KIDS

*GEORGIE &
THE NEW KID*

GRACE STREET KIDS

GEORGIE & THE NEW KID

STANDARD
PUBLISHING
Cincinnati, Ohio

Marti Plemons

Grace Street Kids

Megan & the Owl Tree
Josh & the Guinea Pig
Georgie & the New Kid
Scott & the Ogre

The Standard Publishing Company, Cincinnati, Ohio.
A division of Standex International Corporation.

99 98 97 96 95 94 93 92   5 4 3 2 1

Library of Congress Cataloging-in-Publication Data

Plemons, Marti.
  Georgie & the new kid / Marti Plemons.
    p. cm. — (Grace Street kids)
  Summary: Discovering that the new girl on Grace Street, who has become very
popular and almost taken Georgie's best friend away, has been lying to everyone,
Georgie wonders if she should expose her dishonesty.
  ISBN 0-87403-687-9
  [1. Friendship—Fiction. 2. Honesty—Fiction. 3. Christian life—Fiction.] I. Title.
II. Title: Georgie and the new kid. III. Series: Plemons, Marti. Grace Street kids.
  PZ7.P718Ge 1992
  [Fic]—dc20   91-39318
                                                  CIP
                                                  AC

For Steven

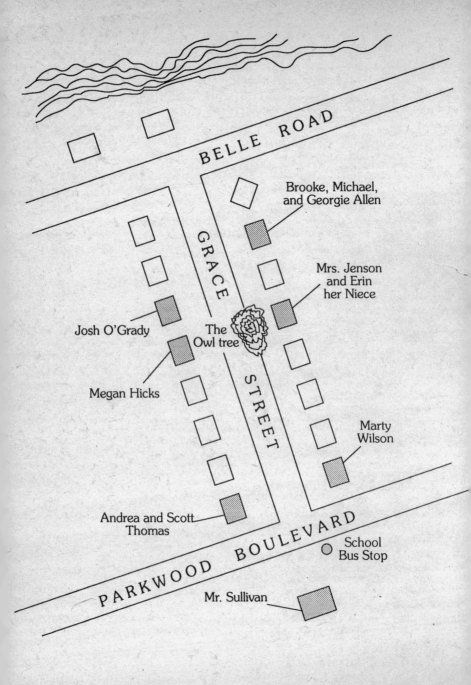

Chapter One

Georgie knelt on her bare knees in Martha Wilson's dining room. She rested her arms on the windowsill and gazed intently across Grace Street at the orange and white moving van. "Think they've got any kids?"

"Two," said Marty, who was crowded in next to her at the window. "Looks like boys . . . no . . . one boy and one girl."

Georgie scanned the Early American furniture

being carried into the house across the street. "How can you tell?"

"The girl's about our age," Marty continued in a mysterious, halting, fortune-teller's voice. "The boy is . . . let's see . . . yes, he's older, but I think . . . yes, he's just a year ahead of us in school."

Georgie stared at her best friend in disbelief. "You can tell all that from their furniture?"

Marty grinned. "Of course not. My dad's their real estate agent."

Georgie shoved her and Marty giggled, letting herself fall over onto the floor. Georgie laughed, too, and sat with her back to the wall beneath the window. Little craters were pressed into her knees from the pattern of the carpet.

"You should have seen your face!"

"I didn't really believe you," argued Georgie, but she was grinning sheepishly.

"Did so."

"OK, *Martha*, maybe I did. So what?" Marty hated being called by her real name.

"Don't Martha me, *Georgiana* Allen!"

They both laughed. In the two years they had been best friends, there had never been a serious argument between them.

"Is she going to be in the fifth grade too?" asked Georgie.

"Who?"

"The new kid. You said she's our age."

"Oh, yeah. I think so. I know her brother's going to be in the sixth."

"So's Michael." Georgie's brother, Michael, was the only other sixth grader on Grace Street, if you didn't count Erin Jenson who only spent the summers there.

"Hey, yeah! He'll finally have somebody to be friends with."

The rumble of a motor made them jump up to look out the window. With a grinding of gears the moving van pulled away from the curb, and Georgie could see a small, brown and white station wagon in the driveway. A boy Michael's age was pulling a large, cardboard box across the tailgate. He was tall, with short, blond hair made dark by the grease that held it in little spikes all over his head. He wore jeans that were faded and torn and a brown leather bomber jacket over a plain white T-shirt.

"Maybe not," said Marty.

"What?"

"I can just see your dad's face if Michael starts hanging out with that guy!"

"Well, that's not fair. We don't even know him yet."

"We know he wears a leather jacket in August. How can he stand it?"

"Your mom wears pantyhose in August. Makeup, too."

"It's not the same thing."

"Why not?"

"Well, she's a nurse."

"So?"

"So . . ." Marty frowned. "OK, maybe it is the same thing."

"Anyway, my dad's not like that."

"Yeah, your dad's pretty cool. Look. There's the girl."

She stood on the front porch holding the screen door open while her brother carried boxes in from the station wagon. Her long, blond hair was pulled back in a ponytail that brushed across her shoulder blades when she turned her head. She was almost as tall as her mother, who came out of the house, propped the door open with a lamp, and ushered her daughter back inside.

Georgie giggled. "I don't think your new neighbor likes to work."

"She seems nice, though."

"Let's go meet her."

"My dad said not to bother them until tomorrow."

"Oh." Georgie sat back on the carpet. "What do you want to do, then?"

"I don't know. What do you want to do?"

"I asked you first."

"We could go to your house and play Parcheesi."

"I'm tired of playing Parcheesi. Let's go to the creek and play Robin Hood."

"I don't want to play Robin Hood. Let's go pester Brooke and Megan."

"They went to the movies."

Brooke, Georgie's older sister, was nice to Georgie most of the time, but when she was with Megan Hicks she acted like she didn't want Georgie around. Georgie couldn't understand why.

Marty sighed. "I'll be glad when school starts."

"Me, too."

They decided to ride their bicycles to the

Mabel Street Market. Marty's house cornered on Parkwood Boulevard, but Georgie wasn't allowed to go that way because of the traffic. They had to ride to the other end of Grace Street, down Belle Road and across Parkwood on Amanda Avenue. When they got to Mabel Street, Georgie spotted a brown and white station wagon parked in front of the market. She slowed until Marty came up beside her.

"Look. They're at the market."

"Marty's pudgy face split into a grin. "Let's go."

They found the woman and her daughter in the dairy aisle selecting a carton of milk. Georgie looked around but didn't see the boy. Marty headed straight for the dairy aisle.

"Hi. I'm Marty Wilson. You just moved in across the street from us."

The woman smiled. "Well, it's nice to meet you, Marty. I'm Rose Thomas. This is my daughter, Andrea."

Andrea smiled. "Hi."

"She's Georgie."

"Georgie Allen," said Georgie. "We live on Grace Street, too."

"Down at the other end," added Marty.

"That's wonderful!" said Mrs. Thomas. "As soon as we're settled you'll both have to come visit Andrea."

Georgie smiled at Andrea, but when Andrea smiled back there was no warmth on her face. Her pale blue eyes stared into Georgie's like a challenge. Georgie looked away.

"Can't I go with them now?" Andrea asked her mom.

"We've got our bicycles," said Georgie.

"We could walk them back," suggested Marty.

"I'm sorry, girls," said Mrs. Thomas, "but I need Andrea at home today."

"That's OK," said Georgie.

"Maybe we'll see you tomorrow," said Marty. Mrs. Thomas smiled warmly. "That would be very nice. You can meet Andrea's brother, Scott. He's going to be sorry, now, that he didn't come to the store with us. Won't he, Andrea?"

Andrea sulked.

When the Thomases left, Georgie and Marty bought ice cream cones and sat on a bench in front of the market to eat them.

"Andrea's pretty," observed Marty.

"Yeah, but she's kind of . . . I don't know . . . fake, or something."

"What do you mean?"

"I don't know, but I don't think I like her."

"Well, that's not fair," mimicked Marty. *"We don't even know her yet."*

Georgie giggled.

"That's what *you* said."

"I know," said Georgie, "but you've got ice cream on your nose."

Marty grinned and wiped her nose.

Georgie knew she wasn't supposed to judge people, but there was something about Andrea that didn't seem right. It wasn't the same as spiked hair and leather jackets. It was something in Andrea's eyes, and it made Georgie feel uncomfortable.

At dinner that night Georgie announced the arrival of the Thomases.

"I don't want you over there getting in their way while they're trying to unpack," cautioned her mom.

"We weren't," said Georgie. "We met them at the market."

"What are they like?" asked Brooke.

"Mrs. Thomas is nice," she said, and added vaguely, "Andrea's my age."

Her dad said, "Mr. Wilson told me there were two children."

"There's a boy, too," said Georgie. "Scott. He's the same age as Michael. We didn't meet him yet, though. We didn't meet Mr. Thomas, either. I guess he was at work or something."

When Georgie's mom got up to clear the table, Georgie helped her. All the dishes had been taken to the kitchen and the leftovers put away before Georgie finally said, "Mom? Can I ask you something?"

"Of course," said her mom over the sound of water running into the sink. Georgie's dad wanted to get them an automatic dishwasher, but her mom wouldn't have it.

"Did you ever, you know, just not like somebody?"

"You mean without a good reason?"

"Yes."

Georgie's mom turned off the water and looked at her. "Why? Do you?"

Georgie nodded.

"Who?"

"Andrea."

"You just met her."

"I know, and Marty liked her. I just . . . didn't."

"Well, maybe you only need some time to get to know her. I'll tell you what. When you say your prayers tonight, say a special one for Andrea. It's hard to keep on not liking someone you've prayed for."

"You really think it'll work?"

"I'm sure of it."

Georgie wasn't so sure, but she decided to try.

Chapter Two

Early the next morning, Georgie walked to Marty's house. She expected to find Marty having breakfast at the kitchen table or maybe still lying in bed—Georgie loved getting there early enough to wake her up—but Marty's mother said she had already gone to Andrea's.

Georgie scuffed slowly across Grace Street to the Thomases'. Mrs. Thomas let her in and showed her to Andrea's room.

"Hi, Georgie," she bubbled. "Did you ever see so many clothes in your whole life?"

Georgie looked at the clothes piled a foot high across every inch of Andrea's full-sized bed and shook her head. "Only in a department store."

"We're picking out school clothes and stuff."

"The closet's too little to hold everything." Andrea pointed to the layers of clothes.

Georgie picked up a pink sweater that was so soft it felt like baby clothes. "What are you going to do with the rest of it?"

"I don't know," said Andrea, snatching the sweater from her hands.

Georgie stared but said nothing.

"Her mom's going to store it in the attic," said Marty, "till next summer."

"I hate this house," said Andrea. "We had a big house before, with lots of closets."

"Why did you move?" asked Georgie.

Andrea gave her a look that said it was none of her business.

Marty didn't seem to notice. "Hey, let's get these clothes sorted out so we can go do something," she said.

"Don't look at me," said Georgie. "She doesn't want me touching her precious clothes."

"That's not what I meant," Andrea told her, glancing at Marty.

"Then what did you mean?" asked Georgie, sounding so much like her father that Marty grinned.

"Well, I just meant . . ."

Georgie grinned, too.

"What's so funny?"

Marty broke into a laugh.

"I don't know," said Georgie, still grinning.

Andrea gave Marty a hurt look. "Are you laughing at me, Marty?"

Marty shook her head and gasped, "No, Georgie."

Georgie giggled, too, and tried to reach Marty with a punch but the bed was between them. Andrea smiled and looked with puzzled eyes from Marty to Georgie.

"*Then what did you mean?*" mimicked Marty. "You sounded just like your dad."

"Did not," said Georgie with a laugh.

"You did so. Here." Marty tossed her a green corduroy jumper. "Hang that up."

Georgie looked at Andrea. Andrea was still wearing that puzzled little smile. *She feels left out,* thought Georgie, and Georgie was glad, sort of, but deep down she felt guilty and knew she should pray for Andrea some more.

After the clothes were sorted, they decided to go to the market for ice cream. When they stopped to get Georgie's bicycle, Andrea met the rest of the Grace Street Kids. Brooke and Megan were in the porch swing playing with Josh O'Grady's guinea pig. Josh lived across the street and one door down, next to Megan. He stood close to the swing and watched.

"Her name's Gizmo," said Josh.

Andrea smiled but kept her distance. Georgie grinned. "We're going to the market," she told Brooke. "Will you tell Mom?"

"I'll go, too," announced Josh, taking Gizmo and dropping his skateboard to the sidewalk.

Andrea back away. "Are you going to take— that?" She nodded toward Gizmo.

Georgie looked at Marty and they smirked when their eyes met. Megan reached for the guinea pig. "I'll take her home," she told Josh.

At the market, Andrea led Marty off to another

aisle, leaving Georgie with Josh. "What grade's she in?" he asked.

"Fifth, but she has a brother about your age."

"Oh." Josh would be in the seventh, with Brooke and Megan.

Georgie eyed Josh. "Why?"

"I just wondered."

Georgie grinned, and Josh blushed to the roots of his fiery red hair. Georgie said, "You think she's cute?"

Josh scowled and walked away. Georgie found Marty and Andrea at the ice cream counter. Andrea was saying, "Thanks. I'll pay you back."

"Hi, Georgie," said Marty. "Where's Josh?"

Georgie grinned. "He's around."

As soon as they got their ice cream, Josh took off. "What's wrong with him?" asked Andrea.

"He's just Josh," said Marty.

Andrea shrugged. "My mom said she'd take us to the mall this afternoon."

"What for?" asked Georgie.

Andrea gave Georgie a look that made her feel as if she had just said the most stupid thing in the world. Georgie blushed, in spite of herself.

Andrea said, "My dad sent me some money."

"Where is your dad?" asked Marty.

"He travels a lot."

"What's he do?" asked Georgie.

"He's a talent agent. He's really important, too, and he has lots of famous clients."

"Wow!" said Marty. "Who?"

"We're not supposed to tell."

"Oh." Marty was disappointed. Georgie doubted the clients were anybody she had ever heard of.

"But he has to be gone a lot," continued Andrea. "That's why we moved out here to this part of town."

"Why?" asked Georgie.

"Because he's gone so much. He thought we'd be safer."

Georgie nodded. "So what are we going to do at the mall?"

"Just stuff," said Andrea. "Don't you guys ever hang out at the mall?"

"That's boring," said Georgie. "Let's go to the creek."

"Marty and I are going to the mall," Andrea told her. "You don't have to come if you don't want to."

"Come on, Georgie," begged Marty. "It'll be fun."

"I don't know."

"Please? Andrea's never been to the mall. We can show her around."

Georgie sighed. "OK. Maybe there'll be something good at the movies."

There wasn't, and Georgie could tell that Andrea had no interest in seeing a movie, anyway. All she wanted to do was try on clothes. Georgie was bored.

"This would look great on you, Georgie," said Andrea, holding a red blouse under Georgie's chin. Black and white pandas played around the hem and down one sleeve.

"Hey, yeah! Try it on, Georgie," urged Marty.

"Come on," said Andrea. "I'll go with you."

"Go on," Marty said. "I'm going to look at shoes a minute."

Reluctantly, Georgie took the blouse and followed Andrea to the dressing room. They found an empty booth and Andrea just stood there, looking like Georgie's mom when she took Georgie shopping for school clothes every fall. Georgie pulled the curtain between them.

After a few minutes, Andrea asked, "How does it look?"

"OK."

"Let's see." Andrea slid the curtain back.

Georgie studied the blouse in the mirror, turning her shoulders so she could see the back. A panda climbed up her spine toward the collar.

"It's great," said Andrea.

"It's OK." Georgie liked it, but she didn't buy it. Maybe she'd bring her mom to see it.

Andrea frowned. "You don't like me, do you, Georgie?"

"I like you," Georgie lied.

Andrea brightened. "Really?"

Georgie couldn't make herself say it again, so she just nodded.

"Good," sighed Andrea, "because Marty's OK, but I'd rather be your friend."

"Why?"

"Well, she's kind of—you know."

"What?"

"She's, you know—fat."

"Marty's not fat."

Andrea giggled. "Well, she's not skinny!"

"That isn't very nice, Andrea. And, anyway, what difference does it make?"

Andrea looked surprised. "I didn't mean anything."

Georgie scowled and closed the curtain.

Chapter Three

Georgie leaned against the giant oak that stood at the edge of Mrs. Jenson's yard. Her oak tree was the place where Georgie and Marty agreed to meet. It was halfway.

"Georgie?" called Mrs. Jenson from her front door.

Georgie still didn't see Marty, so she hurried up to the porch. "Hi, Mrs. Jenson."

"I thought that was you."

"I was waiting for Marty."

"Oh, well, I won't keep you then."

"It's OK. You want me to do something?"

"If you have time. The light's out in the laundry room. Do you think you could climb up and replace the bulb for me? You'll have to stand on the dryer to reach it."

"Sure."

"Oh, good. It won't take a minute. It's just a bare bulb."

Georgie liked helping Mrs. Jenson. The older woman didn't have kids of her own, but her nephew's daughter, Erin, spent the summers there. Erin was a year older that Georgie, but she treated Georgie as if they were the same age.

"I miss Erin already," said Georgie.

"So do I," said Mrs. Jenson, "and she's only been gone a few days."

"Why'd she go back so early? School doesn't start until next week."

"Her mom wanted to take her to Florida first, for a little vacation."

"You should've gone with them."

Mrs. Jenson smiled and tiny lines crinkled

from the corners of her blue-gray eyes to the edge of her silver hair. "Well, they did invite me, but I thought they needed some time alone together."

Georgie thought Erin and her mom were always alone together, but she didn't say so. She just changed Mrs. Jenson's light bulb and said good-bye. She hurried back outside to wait for Marty. Finally, she decided to walk to Marty's house.

"Mrs. Thomas took her and Andrea to the mall," explained Mrs. Wilson. "They were going to pick you up at the oak tree. Didn't you see them?"

Georgie shook her head. She must have been changing the light bulb for Mrs. Jenson.

"I'm sorry, Georgie. Would you like me to take you down there? They haven't been gone long."

"No, thanks."

Georgie walked slowly back up Grace Street. She didn't stop to play with the Dickersons' new baby. She didn't take a detour through Mrs. Jenson's flower garden. She didn't even look to see if Josh was out on his skateboard. She just watched her feet walk home.

When she arrived, her brother Michael was mowing the lawn and Brooke was at her dance class. Georgie went to the creek.

She crossed Belle Road and went through the Ledbetters' rock garden. There was a narrow spot in the creek where stepping stones took her to a small grove of maple trees. Georgie sat on the thick carpet of dark green moss, hugged her knees to her chin, and cried.

"Georgie?" Megan dropped from the limb of a nearby maple and sat next to her. "What's wrong?"

"Nothing," said Georgie, quickly wiping her eyes. "I didn't know you were here."

"It must be something," insisted Megan. "You look like you lost your best friend!"

"Maybe I did."

"Did you and Marty have a fight?"

"No."

"You sure?"

"How could we? She's always with Andrea."

"Oh," said Megan, nodding.

Georgie frowned. It wasn't what she had meant to say. She didn't care if Marty wanted to be friends with someone else. Georgie knew that she was still Marty's best friend. The problem was Andrea.

"What if you knew something?" she asked Megan. "Something that somebody said about another person. But if you told, it would hurt that person's feelings."

"Then I guess you shouldn't tell."

"But if you didn't tell, that person would still think the other person was her friend, and she isn't."

Megan frowned at Georgie. "What are you talking about?"

"I can't tell."

"Well, I can't help if I don't understand what the problem is."

"That's OK," sighed Georgie. "Thanks, anyway."

"Did you pray about it?"

"Yes, but I still don't know what to do."

"Did you listen for an answer?"

"What do you mean?"

"You can't just pray, Georgie, and not listen for an answer."

Georgie had never thought about that before but it made sense. After Megan went home

Georgie sat by the creek and listened. A downy woodpecker hammered out insects while songbirds swapped tunes. Dragonflies hummed over the rustle of maple leaves in the summer breeze. The creek gurgled and cooed like a happy baby. But Georgie didn't hear any answers.

On the Thursday before Labor Day every year, Georgie's mom took the whole family shopping for school clothes and supplies. Most stores were already having their back-to-school sales, but the crowds weren't as bad as they would be on the weekend. Crowds or no crowds, Georgie hated it.

"Georgie, we go through this every year," said her mom. "You're coming with us, and I don't want to hear another word about it."

"Just put your shoes on and let's get it over with," grumbled Michael.

Georgie's mom said, "Honestly, you'd think I was forcing you to wrestle tigers or something!"

"*Wrestle tigers*, Mom?" asked Michael, rolling his eyes.

"I like to go shopping," announced Brooke. Georgie glared at her.

It wasn't so bad once they got to the mall. Even the red blouse with pandas was on sale, and Georgie's mom bought it for her. At noon, her mom deposited Georgie and Michael and all their packages at a table in the food fair and went off with Brooke to look for dance leotards. Georgie sighed.

"Michael?"

"What?" he mumbled around a mouth full of chicken.

"Never mind." Georgie pinched off little bits of her sandwich bun and dropped them on her plate.

"What's the matter?"

"Nothing."

"Yes there is. You're leaving bread crumbs."

Georgie put her sandwich on her plate and her hands in her lap. She looked at Michael. "Do you like Andrea?"

"Don't be stupid."

"I don't mean *like* her. I just mean, you know, what do you think of her?"

"Oh. I don't know. She's OK, I guess."

"Yeah. That's what everybody thinks."

"Don't you like her?"

"No."

"Why not? Because she likes Marty? Or because Marty likes her?"

Georgie glared at her brother. "Neither one. It's because she *doesn't* like Marty, but she acts like she does."

"How do you know?"

"She told me."

"Are you going to tell Marty?"

"It would hurt her feelings."

"Yeah, but Marty'd quit hanging out with her."

"You think I should tell her?"

"Uh-uh. You're not getting me in this," said Michael, shaking his head emphatically. "Are you going to eat that sandwich?"

Georgie shoved what was left of her sandwich across the table and stood up. "I'm going to go find Mom."

"Tell her to hurry, OK?"

Georgie walked along the mall toward the hosiery store, stopping now and then to look at a book or a card or a pair of shoes. It wasn't that she didn't like shopping, but Brooke's idea of shopping was trying on clothes. Come to think of it, that was Andrea's idea, too. Georgie just didn't care that much about clothes.

At the pet store, Georgie watched a litter of kittens tumble and play while one fuzzy yellow sibling slept peacefully in its water bowl. When she turned to leave, Georgie noticed a crowd gathering in front of the dress shop next door. Curious, she tried to push closer but a security guard stood in the way.

"What's happening?" asked Georgie just as the guard hurried on into the store.

Georgie slipped around and squeezed in beside the window. Inside she saw the security guard talking to the manager. With them were two sales clerks and a girl with blond hair that fell to the middle of her back. Georgie tugged at a woman's sleeve.

"What's going on?" she asked her.

The woman shrugged. "It looks like they caught that kid shoplifting."

Georgie looked at the girl. She seemed small and frightened as she turned to speak to the security guard. When she saw the girl's face, Georgie gasped. It was Andrea Thomas.

Chapter Four

Where's Andrea?" asked Brooke.

"She has to stay home and help her mom," said Marty, "but I invited Scott to go with us."

The Grace Street Kids were going to the movies. They had gathered in Megan's driveway and were waiting for Mrs. Hicks to take them to the theater. Georgie watched Josh guide his skateboard through big, lazy figure eights and asked casually, "What's she helping her mom do?"

"I don't know," said Marty. "She didn't say."

"Well, whatever it is," complained Brooke, "I don't see why her mom couldn't give her a couple hours off to go to the movies with us."

Marty spied Andrea's brother. "There's Scott," she said.

The kids watched silently as Scott wound his way up the gently curving Grace Street sidewalk. When he reached Megan's driveway, Georgie introduced him to everyone. Her brother ignored the spiked hair and leather jacket and zeroed in on the hundred-and-fifty-dollar high-tops on his feet. Michael was impressed.

"Hey, cool!" he exclaimed. "Where'd you get those?"

Scott shrugged. "My dad."

Georgie grinned. She saw Josh looking at the shoes but pretending not to. *He's impressed, too,* she thought, and Josh didn't impress easily.

Marty said, "You think if we call your mom she'll change her mind and let Andrea come with us?"

Scott shook his head. "No way. Besides, Mom doesn't like us to call her at work."

"Your mom's at work?" asked Georgie.

"Yeah. I can't go, either. That's what I came to tell you."

"That's not fair," pouted Brooke.

"I know," said Scott. "Andrea's the one who's grounded, but I have to stay home with her."

"Andrea's grounded?" asked Georgie. "What did she do?"

Scott shrugged. "Something about when she went to the mall yesterday."

Georgie hadn't told anyone what she had seen at the dress shop. If she told them now, they'd know she'd been right about Andrea all along. Marty's parents might even find out and forbid Marty to play with Andrea ever again. But when Georgie opened her mouth, she discovered she couldn't say anything. Something was telling her not to.

On Labor Day, Georgie's dad organized a cookout so the Thomases could meet their Grace Street neighbors. Georgie wasn't the only one surprised when she saw Andrea.

"I thought you were grounded," said Josh bluntly.

"Mom suspended it for the cookout."

Josh persisted. "What'd you do, anyway?"

"Shut up, Josh," said Marty. "It's none of our business."

"That's OK, Marty," said Andrea. "It's no big deal. I just went to the mall without asking first."

Georgie looked up quickly. "She lets you go to the mall all the time. How come you didn't ask?"

"She was at work," explained Andrea. "Besides, I didn't think she'd find out."

"How *did* she find out?"

Andrea shrugged. "I guess Scotty told her."

Georgie looked at Scott sitting by himself at the edge of the deck. He hadn't even known what the grounding was for. Georgie knew Andrea was lying, just as she had lied about being grounded in the first place, but Georgie didn't say anything. She didn't know why. She just couldn't. She crossed the yard to where her dad was tending the barbecue grill.

"Hi, Daddy."

"Hi, there, Georgie Porgie. What's up?"

"Nothing, why?"

"Well, for one thing, you're over here talking to me instead of playing with your friends."

Georgie watched him turn a steak on the grill,

sliding it in between a pork chop and a hot dog. Each family had brought their own meat, so there were steaks and pork chops, hamburgers and hot dogs, beef and pork ribs, various chicken parts, and something that looked like a flattened hockey puck.

"What's that?" asked Georgie.

"Beef liver."

"Yuck! Don't let it touch my hamburger!"

Her dad grinned. "Don't worry. I've got it quarantined!"

Georgie laughed.

"How're we doing here, Allen?" asked Mr. Hicks, striding up to the grill and clapping Georgie's dad on the back.

"We'll talk later, Georgie," said Mr. Allen. "OK?"

Georgie nodded.

"Am I interrupting something?" asked Mr. Hicks.

"It's OK," said Georgie.

She found the kids sprawled across the deck talking about school. Josh was leaning against the railing with his feet resting on his skateboard, rolling it gently back and forth across the redwood planks. "Mr. Prescott's the worst," he was saying, "but you can't escape him. He teaches all the science."

"Do you change classes in the sixth grade?" asked Scott.

"Just for science and P.E.," said Megan. "And I *like* Mr. Prescott."

"Yeah, but you like science," said Brooke. "I thought he was hard."

Georgie laughed. "*You* thought Mrs. Leatherby was hard!"

Megan explained to Scott and Andrea, "Mrs. Leatherby's the nicest teacher in the sixth grade."

"Easiest, you mean," said Georgie, "probably in the whole school."

"How would you know?" asked Brooke.

"Everybody knows."

Michael said, "Well, I don't care who I get."

"Me neither," said Andrea, "as long as Marty and I are in the same class. And Georgie, too," she added quickly.

"Georgie and I have been in the same class every year, haven't we, Georgie?" asked Marty.

"So far."

She and Marty had been friends at school even

before Georgie's family moved to Grace Street.
Marty's dad had sold them their house. Suddenly, Georgie grinned. "I bet it was your dad
that brought the liver!"

Marty laughed. "How'd you know?"

"Who else would bring beef liver to a cookout?"

"My dad would," said Andrea.

"Barbecued beef liver?" asked Brooke with a
shudder.

"Yum," said Josh, rubbing his stomach and
licking his lips.

"Yuck," said Michael.

"It's good," said Andrea. "My dad eats stuff
like that all the time."

"Her dad's a talent agent for some really
famous people," Marty informed them.

"Who told you that?" asked Scott.

Marty looked uncertainly at Andrea. "Isn't
that what you said?"

"Sure," said Andrea. "We can tell that part,
Scotty. We just can't tell any names."

"Where is your dad?" asked Josh, his green
eyes searching the clusters of grown-ups
crowded into the Allen's backyard.

"He couldn't come," said Andrea. "He loves cookouts, but he travels a lot."

Georgie glanced at Scott. He was glaring at Andrea, but she either didn't see him or didn't care.

"He's going to take us with him," she continued, "the next time he goes to California. He said we could go to Disneyland."

Scott got up and walked away, the heels of his boots clicking angrily across the deck.

"Where're you going?" asked Josh.

"I'm hungry," Scott growled as he headed for the barbecue grill.

The cookout lasted until after dark. Georgie and Michael helped clean up the backyard while Brooke went inside to help with the dishes. When Michael took the folding chairs to the garage, Georgie went over to where her dad was cleaning the grill.

"Here, hold this," he said, handing her the nozzle end of the garden hose.

Georgie took the hose and twisted the nozzle back and forth in her hands, making a fine spray of water appear and disappear in the air.

"OK," said her dad, "let's have it."

Georgie twisted the nozzle open and directed a steady stream of water at the grill. Her dad jumped back.

"Not the water!" he shouted.

"Sorry," mumbled Georgie, closing the nozzle quickly.

Her dad laughed. "I meant for you to tell me what's been on your mind all day."

Georgie grinned. "Oh, that."

"Yeah, that."

"Well, it's Andrea," began Georgie and stopped, thinking about what she wanted to say.

"Yes," prompted her dad, "what about her?"

"Well, she's not a very nice person."

"Oh? What brings you to that conclusion?"

"See, that's just it," said Georgie. "Whenever I try to tell anybody, I just can't, for some reason."

"You mean you don't know why you feel the way you do about her?"

"No. I mean, yes, I do know why. I just don't know if I should tell."

"I see. Have you prayed about this?"

"Yes, and I've been listening for an answer."

Georgie's dad smiled proudly at her. "Good girl. Let's have some water now—but slowly!"

Georgie opened the nozzle halfway and let the water run gently across the grill.

"You know what I think," said her dad. "If you're having trouble telling what you know about Andrea, maybe that's your answer."

Georgie frowned. "What's my answer?"

"Maybe God is telling you to keep quiet."

That's what Georgie was afraid of. She had asked God to tell her what to do about Andrea. What she had wanted was for Andrea to mess up in front of everybody. Then they would all know, but Georgie wouldn't have to be the one to tell them. The last thing she wanted was for God to tell her to keep it to herself!

"You know, Georgie," said her dad, "judging people by the way they act is just as wrong as judging them by the way they look."

"But if you can't judge people by what they do, how are you supposed to judge them?"

Georgie's dad looked at her with surprise. "You know the answer to that, Georgie. The Bible says we're not to judge people at all."

Chapter Five

The school bus stopped at the Parkwood Boulevard end of Grace Street. Mornings, the kids had to cross the busy two-lane street and wait on the sidewalk in front of Mr. Sullivan's house.

"And you better not stick a toe in the old snake's yard, either," said Josh, "or he'll cut it off and keep it for a souvenir!"

"No he won't," said Andrea, but shot a glance at the white brick house with the black shutters.

"He will, too," insisted Josh. "He's got a whole collection of kids' toes hanging on the wall in his living room. I saw it through the window."

"Stop it, Josh," said Megan, putting a protective arm around her little sister, Amy.

Georgie grinned. Amy was in the first grade, and she was riding the bus for the first time. She hugged against Megan's side clutching a brand-new pink backpack with lavender straps.

"What's in your backpack, Amy?" asked Georgie.

"Lunch," said Amy proudly. "Peanut butter and jelly."

When the bus came, Andrea pushed in front of Georgie and managed to share a seat with Marty. Georgie had to sit near the front with a girl she didn't know. At school, she and Marty were put into separate classes the first time in five years.

"I can't believe it," complained Marty. "It's not fair!"

"I know," said Georgie, "but there's nothing we can do about it."

"And anyway," said Andrea brightly, "you've still got me." Andrea was assigned to Marty's class.

Georgie didn't see them until lunchtime. She carried her tray to their table but there were so many kids huddled around Andrea, listening to stories about her fabulous father and his famous clients, that Georgie couldn't find a place to sit.

"I thought you were going to save me a seat," she accused Marty before walking away without giving her a chance to reply.

Georgie found an empty table in the corner and sat down. Marty slipped into the chair across from her. "I'm sorry, Georgie," she began. "I tried to save a seat, but . . ."

"Yeah, right," Georgie interrupted sarcastically. Marty looked hurt. Georgie tried not to notice. "You better hurry back to your new friend," she told her. "She might get lonely without you."

"Why are you so mad at me?"

"Why don't you want me around anymore?"

Marty's blue eyes widened. "I don't! I mean, I do want you around. You're my best friend!"

Georgie gave in. "I know. It's not your fault. It's Andrea."

"Andrea wants you around," said Marty. "She

said she wants to be friends with you, but she thinks you don't like her."

"She's right."

"But why, Georgie? She's so nice."

"Maybe she's not as nice as you think she is."

"What do you mean?"

Georgie was about to tell her, in spite of the nagging little voice saying not to, but she spotted Andrea coming toward them. "Never mind."

All the fifth-grade classes went to P.E. at the same time. Mr. Kimsey took the boys to the softball field, and Miss Arvin selected team captains for volleyball. Andrea was the second one selected. Georgie sighed. The captains got to take turns picking players for their teams. Andrea would pick Marty and Georgie would be left out again.

"Georgie Allen," said Andrea on her very first call.

When Georgie went to stand behind Andrea, Marty was smiling. When Andrea's second call came and Andrea didn't pick her, Marty's smile became just a little puzzled.

After two more calls, Georgie leaned close to Andrea's ear and whispered, "Pick Marty."

But Andrea ignored Marty and picked someone else. Suddenly Andrea's words rang in
Georgie's memory. *She's, you know — fat.*

Georgie shoved her elbow into Andrea's side
and nodded toward Marty. Miss Arvin frowned
at Georgie, just as Andrea finally said, "Marty
Wilson."

After school, Georgie let Andrea board the bus
ahead of her, then slid into the seat behind her.
When Marty got on, she sat next to Georgie.
Andrea turned sideways and looked at them
across the back of the seat.

"How come nobody wants to sit with me?"

"We are sitting with you," said Georgie.

"No you're not," pouted Andrea. "You're
back there, and I'm up here all by myself." She
looked sweetly at Marty. "Will you come sit
with me?"

"Then I'd be by myself," Georgie pointed out.

"Besides," said Marty, "I was with you all day.
Oh, Georgie, I wish you were in our class, too."

"Who wants to go to the store when we get
home?" asked Andrea.

"What store?" asked Georgie. She was in no
mood for going to the mall.

"You know, that little store where we get ice cream."

"Oh, you mean the market," Marty told her.

"Market, store, whatever," said Andrea. "Who wants to go?"

"Aren't you grounded?" asked Georgie.

"That was just till school started."

"I'll go," said Marty. "You coming, Georgie?"

Georgie shrugged. "Yeah, OK." It was better than the mall.

Georgie took her books to her room and let Brooke know where she was going. Her mom taught at Woodmont High School and wouldn't be home for another hour. As usual, Brooke gave her a hard time before telling her she could go.

The three girls rode their bikes to the Mabel Street Market. As they took their ice cream to the counter to pay for it, Andrea borrowed the money for hers from Marty.

Georgie was surprised. "If your dad gives you so much money, how come you don't have enough for ice cream?"

Andrea's pretty face grew bright red as she stared into Georgie's dark eyes. Georgie didn't care. She thought Andrea was taking advantage

of Marty, and she wasn't going to let her get away with it. Georgie held her eyes steady and waited for an answer. Andrea finally gave in.

"He does send us money," she insisted, "but Mom makes us put most of it in the bank. I spent the rest at the mall last week."

"It's OK," said Marty. "I don't mind loaning you some."

"Thanks, I'll pay you back. And when my dad gets home from his trip, I'll ask him to take us someplace. Did I tell you he can get free concert tickets?"

"Really?" asked Marty.

"Yeah, and it doesn't even have to be one of his clients."

"That's great!" said Marty.

"Yeah, great," said Georgie without enthusiasm.

"Andrea!" Scott's voice carried sharply across the store and Andrea jumped like she'd been shot.

"Hi, Scotty."

"You better get on your bicycle and go home—now!" he told her.

Andrea took a deep breath and stood up

straight. "You can't tell me what to do. You're not my father."

"I don't care what you do, but if Mom finds out you broke your grounding you'll get another week."

"You're still grounded?" asked Georgie.

Andrea ignored her and said to Scott, "She won't find out if you don't tell her."

"I'm not going to tell her," said Scott, "but she'll find out."

"What do you mean? How will she find out?"

Scott was already walking away, but over his shoulder he said, "Just don't say I didn't warn you."

"You lied," said Georgie. "You broke your grounding, and we helped. My dad'll kill me!"

"How's he going to know?" asked Andrea.

"He'll know," said Georgie.

"Well, if he gets mad, I'll just tell him the truth. He'll know it wasn't your fault," said Andrea.

"You will?"

"Sure."

Georgie was amazed. Andrea had lied, but she was willing to admit it to Georgie's dad so Georgie wouldn't get into trouble. It was the right thing to do, and the last thing Georgie expected from Andrea. Suddenly, Georgie realized she was still judging Andrea, and she silently asked God to forgive her.

"We'd better go home," suggested Marty.

"I thought we were going to get some ice cream," said Andrea calmly, but once they had their ice cream cones she didn't seem so sure of herself. "Maybe we should go back the short way."

"You mean Parkwood Boulevard?" asked Georgie.

"Yeah, why not?"

"We're not allowed," said Georgie. "That's why not."

"But it's lots closer."

Georgie shook her head. "I can't."

"Me neither," said Marty, "but we could start back now and eat our ice cream on the way instead of eating it here."

Andrea reluctantly agreed, but the melting ice cream slowed them down so much that they didn't really save any time. Georgie could have told them that would happen, but she hadn't felt like arguing about it. By the time they turned the corner onto Grace Street, the sticky, melting ice cream bar was all over her hand and she was wishing she had said something.

"Oh, no!" cried Andrea. She stopped so suddenly that Georgie almost skidded into the back of her bicycle.

"What's wrong?" asked Georgie.

Andrea didn't answer. She was gazing down the street at her house. Georgie looked, too, and her stomach lurched as if she were the one about to be in big trouble. Mrs. Thomas' brown and white station wagon was parked in the driveway.

Chapter Six

Georgie met Marty at the Wilsons' house the next morning, and they waited on the corner for Andrea. "Brooke knew about it when I got home yesterday," said Georgie. "Mrs. Thomas called to see if Andrea was there."

"Did she tell your dad?"

"What do you think?"

"Was he mad?"

"No, but I can't play with Andrea—*at all*—as long as she's grounded."

Andrea spotted them from her front door and ran across the street to join them. Together they crossed Parkwood Boulevard to wait for the bus.

"Well?" urged Marty. "What happened?"

"She came home early," said Andrea.

"That was pretty obvious," Georgie said dryly. "What did she say?"

Andrea shrugged. "The usual. I'm grounded for another week." Marty sighed sympathetically.

Georgie had a hard time feeling sorry for her. After all, Andrea had brought it on herself. She broke her grounding and ran the risk of getting them all in trouble for some stupid ice cream.

"What makes me mad," said Andrea, "is that Scott knew. Mom called home before she left the office and told him she'd be early."

"He came to the market to warn you," Georgie reminded her.

"He *could* have told on you when she called," said Marty.

Andrea looked betrayed. She pouted until the bus came, and didn't even complain when Marty sat with Georgie. "I didn't mean to make her mad," whispered Marty.

"She'll get over it," said Georgie.

Mr. Prescott had an extra large class for science lab. They met in a big double room and sat on stools at long counters with black tops and little chrome sinks along the middle. When Georgie entered the lab, she saw Marty jumping up and down at the back of the room, trying to get her attention. Georgie hurried down the aisle and found an empty seat across the counter from her and Andrea.

"This is great!" said Marty.

Georgie smiled in agreement and looked at Andrea. "You still mad?"

"About what?" asked Andrea innocently.

Mr. Prescott announced a field trip and gave them permission slips to have signed by their parents.

"A pond?" whispered Andrea. "What kind of field trip is that?"

"It'll be fun," Georgie told her. "Michael said they catch frogs and look at moss and leaves and stuff. His class even found a snake!"

"Yuck! I'm not going," said Andrea, wrinkling up her nose.

"It was just a green snake," said Georgie.

"I don't care if it was purple! I'm still not going."

"He makes you write a paper if you don't go."

Andrea looked at Marty, who nodded. Andrea sighed and put the consent form in her notebook.

The field trip took place the following Friday. Andrea's first day of freedom after her second grounding. Gathered in clumps beside the buses, clutching sack lunches and buzzing excitedly, Georgie's science class waited impatiently for Mr. Prescott. Finally, he emerged from the building, his hands full of papers, and called them to order.

"All right, people. Quiet, please, I want one double line."

Georgie sidestepped and stood next to Marty. Andrea slipped around and stood on the other side of Georgie. Mr. Prescott gave them a hard look.

"A *double* line," he repeated. "Do we all understand that double means two? I want you in pairs."

Georgie whispered to Andrea, "Move back."

"You move back."

"I was here first."

Mr. Prescott strolled down the line and stopped beside Andrea. He motioned her to the side and announced, "Andrea needs a partner." Half a dozen volunteers stepped forward.

"Miss popularity," mumbled Georgie.

"You still don't like her, do you?" asked Marty.

"I can't help it."

"Well, you're the only one."

"They don't like her," said Georgie. "They just want some of those free concert tickets she's always bragging about."

Marty frowned, and Georgie was immediately sorry for what she had said. Not judging people was a lot harder than it seemed.

Mr. Prescott finally got them into one double line and told them to stay with their partners all day. "Sit with your partner on the bus. Eat lunch with your partner. Explore the pond with your partner. You are responsible for your buddy. If he or she so much as stubs a toe, it's your responsibility to come and tell me about it. Does everyone understand?"

Georgie put her hand over her mouth to hold in a giggle.

Marty whispered, "What's so funny?"

"Don't sneeze," said Georgie, "or I'll have to go tell Mr. Prescott." Marty snickered. Georgie faked a sneeze, and Marty laughed. Mr. Prescott clapped his hands.

"OK, people. Everybody on the bus."

Marty tried to save the seat in front of them for Andrea and her buddy, Kathy Tucker, but Andrea wouldn't even look their way when she boarded the bus.

"Don't worry about it," said Georgie.

"This isn't going to be any fun if she's going to stay mad at us all day."

"It's me she's mad at, not you."

"She acts like she's mad at both of us."

Georgie sighed. "OK. When we get there we'll swap buddies so she can be with you."

Marty looked surprised. "I don't want to swap buddies."

"If we don't, she'll stay mad."

"Then let her," said Marty decisively. "If she wants to act like a big baby, that's her problem, not mine!"

"Way to go Marty!" said Georgie, almost shouting. Then she scooted down in her seat to hide from Mr. Prescott. When Marty laughed,

Georgie laughed, too. Andrea looked around, but Georgie pretended not to notice.

It didn't take long, after reaching the pond, for Andrea to realize that pouting wasn't getting her anywhere. By the time Mr. Prescott had them walking along the edge of the water, she and Kathy were tagging behind Georgie and Marty.

"Let me know if you see any snakes," Andrea said to Georgie.

"I thought you didn't like snakes."

"I don't! That's why I want to know if you see any!"

Georgie laughed and Andrea seemed pleased. Tiny feelings of guilt started tugging at Georgie's conscience. All Andrea really wanted was somebody to be friends with. Georgie would feel the same way if she moved to a new house in a new neighborhood and had to go to a new school. She decided to try harder to like Andrea, and she silently asked God to help her.

The class ate lunch at the picnic area near the pond. All morning Mr. Prescott had talked about frogs eating insects, snakes eating frogs, birds eating snakes, until Georgie's tuna fish sandwich didn't seem very appetizing.

"You're not supposed to eat tuna, anyway," said Andrea.

"Why not?" asked Kathy, munching happily on her cheese and crackers.

"Because of the dolphins," explained Marty.

"But this tuna was caught with nets that don't drown dolphins," said Georgie.

"How do you know?" asked Andrea.

"It said so on the can."

"Oh. Well, you can eat it, then."

Georgie lifted a corner of the bread and peeked at the tuna. Curling her upper lip, she pushed the sandwich away and shoved a potato chip into her mouth.

"What's wrong?" asked Marty.

"I keep thinking about fish eating pond scum," said Georgie.

"Yuck!" said Andrea. "Did you have to say that?"

Georgie grinned. "You want my tuna, Andrea?"

"No!"

Georgie picked up her sandwich and held it under Andrea's nose. "Ummm. Good old pond-scummy fish!"

Andrea pushed her hand away, but Georgie noticed she was grinning. Georgie smiled and plopped the sandwich on the table in front of Marty.

"Here, Marty. You eat it."

"No way!" Giggling too, Marty slid the sandwich away from her with the tip of one finger.

"I thought Marty would eat anything," laughed Andrea.

Georgie looked at Marty's face and all the giggles left her. Suddenly, Andrea was the only one laughing.

"What's wrong?" Andrea asked.

"That wasn't a very nice thing to say," Georgie told her.

"I was just kidding," said Andrea. "You're not mad, are you Marty."

"It's OK," Marty mumbled down the front of her shirt, but Georgie was afraid she was going to cry.

"It's not OK," said Georgie. "It was mean."

Andrea looked genuinely surprised. "Hey, I'm sorry. It wasn't supposed to be mean."

Marty tried to smile. "You better go tell Mr. Prescott, Georgie."

"Tell him what?"

"Your buddy got her feelings hurt. It's your responsibility to go tell him!"

Georgie smiled. What a sport that Marty was! Soon they were all laughing again, and Marty seemed to forget about Andrea's remark. After lunch, Kathy slipped on the bank and fell into the pond. She wasn't hurt, but Andrea had to run and tell Mr. Prescott. All the kids sympathized with Kathy and treated Andrea like a hero.

"You'd think she saved her life, or something," grumbled Georgie.

"Next time, *I* get the clumsy buddy!" said Marty.

Georgie grinned. "Do you want me to go fall in?"

"I've got a better idea," giggled Marty. "I'll be Andrea's buddy and you can push *her* in!"

Georgie laughed. Inside, though, she knew Marty's feelings were still hurt, and it made her sad.

On Saturday, when Andrea wanted to go to the mall, Marty went to the creek with Georgie instead. Sunday afternoon the three of them rode

their bikes to the market again, and Marty took only enough money for her own ice cream. Georgie felt awkward eating in front of Andrea, so she bought two small cups and shared with her.

Monday morning Marty met Georgie at the sidewalk, and they walked to Parkwood Boulevard. Marty started checking the traffic to cross.

"Don't you want to wait for Andrea?" asked Georgie.

"We can wait for her at the bus stop."

"Are you mad at her?"

"No. Why?"

Georgie didn't answer. When the traffic cleared, they ran across the street. Georgie's foot was on the curb when she heard Andrea calling.

"Hey, wait for me!"

Georgie turned and watched. It was all she could do. She saw Andrea running toward Parkwood Boulevard. She saw the red truck with the black mud flaps. A split second before it actually happened, her mind told her Andrea wouldn't make it across the intersection. Tires squealed. Andrea didn't even scream.

Chapter Seven

"Thank God he wasn't speeding," said Marty's mom. "She might have been killed."

Georgie looked at the man who had been driving the truck. He was sitting half in and half out of a police car, his feet resting on the pavement, elbows on his knees, and his head cradled in his hands. He didn't look much older than Marty's brother who was away at college.

"Are they going to arrest him?" she asked Mrs. Wilson.

"No, sweetheart. They know it was an accident."

Georgie said a silent prayer for him. She had already prayed for Andrea when the ambulance took her away to the hospital.

"Can we go to the hospital?" asked Marty.

"Well, I have the evening shift this week," said her mom. "I could pick you up after school on my way to work."

"Do we have to go to school?"

"You certainly do."

"But, Mom . . ."

"It will help take your mind off what's happened. Besides, the hospital won't let you see her for a while, anyway."

"But you work there."

"Marty, I'll take you this afternoon."

"Me, too?" asked Georgie.

"Sure. I'll call your mom. Maybe she can give you both a ride home from the hospital."

Georgie felt better. Marty's mom always seemed to know what to do. She had seen the accident from her window, called 911, and run out to check Andrea for broken bones before Georgie could even make her feet move from the spot where she'd been standing. Andrea had been conscious but seemed to be in shock.

After the ambulance arrived, Mrs. Wilson had taken Scott home to call his mom and then returned with him to the bus stop. Scott's mom had told him to ride the bus to school and wait for her in the office there.

The bus was late. Georgie could see its bright yellow top stuck in traffic about two blocks away. By the time the police cars got out of the way and the traffic started moving again, the bus was already twenty minutes late for school.

"Do the teachers get mad when the whole bus is late?" asked Georgie.

Mrs. Wilson smiled and patted Georgie on the shoulder. "Everything's going to be fine," she told her. "So you can stop worrying, OK?"

"OK."

Mrs. Wilson kissed Georgie on the forehead, hugged and kissed Marty, and watched them get on the bus. It was the quietest bus ride Georgie had ever taken, and the longest day she had ever spent at school. When the last bell finally rang, Marty's mom was waiting for them.

"I called the duty nurse," she told them. "Andrea's got a broken arm and some pretty bad bruises, but she's going to be just fine."

Georgie and Marty grinned at each other.

"They'll let you see her," continued Mrs. Wilson, "but you can only stay a few minutes."

"How come?" asked Marty.

"Because they're giving her medication for the pain and she's going to be very groggy."

"Does she have a cast on her arm?" asked Georgie.

"I'm sure she does."

"Can we sign it?"

Mrs. Wilson laughed. "I guess that's up to her."

Andrea was on the children's ward in a big room with two rows of beds. Georgie saw Mrs. Thomas first, sitting in a chair beside Andrea's bed reading a paperback book. She stood up when Georgie and Marty approached.

"Hello, girls." Her voice was soft but not quite a whisper. It reminded Georgie of the library, or church.

"Hi, Mrs. Thomas," said Georgie using the same, hushed tone. "How's Andrea?"

"She's sleeping."

Georgie looked at the bed. Andrea seemed small and pale against the starched, white pillows. She had a large, purple bruise on the right side of her face and a cast that covered her left arm from shoulder to knuckles.

"Andrea?" Mrs. Thomas called gently, stroking Andrea's cheek. Her eyes fluttered open. "Honey, look who's here. It's Marty and Georgie."

"Hi," said Georgie.

Andrea smiled weakly.

Marty said, "I'm sorry, Andrea."

"For what?"

"We should have waited for you. Georgie wanted to. It was my fault."

"Wasn't your fault," Andrea managed to say before her eyes closed again.

"Of course, it wasn't your fault," said Mrs. Thomas. "You just stop thinking like that, you understand?"

Marty nodded. Georgie stared at her. All day long Marty had felt guilty about Andrea's accident and Georgie hadn't even known.

"We'd better go," said Marty.

"Yeah," agreed Georgie, "my mom's picking us up."

"Thank you for coming, girls."

"We'll come back tomorrow," promised Georgie.

They were allowed to stay longer the next day. Andrea was sitting up eating Jell-O and reading comic books when they arrived.

A stuffed Saint Bernard, taller than Georgie, sat looking at her from the foot of the bed.

"My dad gave him to me," said Andrea. "His name's Bruno."

"Hi, Bruno," said Georgie, running her fingers through the velvety brown fur. "Are you a good dog?"

Andrea grinned. "Except he won't eat my Jell-O for me!"

Georgie and Marty chuckled. Andrea laughed and winced holding her left side with her right hand. "Don't," she begged, her voice coming in little catches. "Don't—make me—laugh. It—hurts!"

"Sorry," said Marty.

"You did it," Georgie told Andrea.

"Uh-uh," said Andrea, shaking her head. "Bruno did it."

They all laughed again, punctuated every few seconds by a pained "Oh!" from Andrea. Finally, there was an awkward silence and their smiles faded.

"I guess that was pretty stupid, wasn't it?" said Andrea.

"What?"

"Running out in the street like that."

"Yeah, I guess it was," said Georgie.

"We should have waited for you," said Marty.

"It wasn't your fault," said Andrea. "Even Amy knows how to cross the street!"

Georgie looked at Bruno. "So your dad's home?"

"No, he's . . ." Andrea hesitated as tears welled up in her eyes. "He'll come when he can, though. And he sent Bruno."

Georgie thought about the time she had fallen off the deck and had to have stitches above her eye. Her dad was speaking at a convention in the city, but he'd left in the middle of his own workshop to meet them at the emergency room.

"You won't believe what my mom did," said Marty.

Georgie grinned. "Marty was *so* embarrassed!"

Andrea brightened. "What? Tell me."

"When I got to Marty's house this morning," said Georgie, "there was Mrs. Wilson, standing on the corner."

Andrea frowned. "So?"

"So, she made us wait to cross the street until she checked to make sure it was safe!" said Marty.

"And not just us," added Georgie. "All the kids. Even Josh."

"Then she stood there," said Marty, "until the bus drove away!"

"Oh, no!" exclaimed Andrea.

"She did," confirmed Georgie. "I thought Marty was going to die."

"What's even worse," said Marty glumly, "is that she's going to do it every day!"

"For how long?"

"Till I don't have any friends left," predicted Marty.

"You'll always have us," said Andrea. "Won't she, Georgie?"

"Sure," agreed Georgie, "and Bruno!"

When Georgie got home she told Brooke and Michael how well Andrea was doing. When her dad got home, she told it all over again. Then, impulsively, she gave him a big hug.

"Thank you, Georgie Porgie. What's that for?"

"I'm just glad you're you," said Georgie.

Her dad smiled. "Any particular reason?"

Georgie shrugged. "Andrea's dad sent her a dog."

"He did?"

Georgie nodded. "A great big stuffed Saint Bernard."

"Well, that was nice of him."

"But he didn't come to see her."

Mr. Allen leaned forward in his chair and rested his elbows on his knees. "These things are hard for everybody, Georgie. I'm sure he wanted to be there."

"I know, but if you were away on a trip and I was in the hospital, you'd come home."

"People are different."

"But he never comes to anything. He didn't come to the cookout. He didn't even help them move!"

"Well, honey, that's what it means to be divorced. Your family's not together anymore."

"Divorced!" Georgie was sure he must have said something that only sounded like that word.

Her dad gave her a curious look. "Didn't you know?"

"Andrea said her dad was on a business trip."

"He may be. I don't know. But I do know that Andrea's parents are divorced."

Chapter Eight

Divorced?" Georgie nodded.

"That's what my dad said."

Marty hugged her books against her and chewed thoughtfully at the corner of her lip. "But why didn't she tell us?"

"I don't know."

They were sitting on Marty's front steps. Mrs. Wilson was standing bus duty on the corner, and Georgie could tell she was watching them. Finally, after all the other Grace Street kids had crossed Parkwood Boulevard, she came back down the sidewalk toward them.

"You're going to be late, girls."

Marty and Georgie walked out to meet her.

"I don't want anybody having to run for the bus."

"We're coming," said Georgie.

"Can we go see Andrea again this afternoon?" asked Marty.

"Yes," her mom told her, "but not at the hospital. Andrea's coming home today!"

After school Georgie dumped her books at Marty's house and they crossed Grace Street to visit Andrea.

"What are you going to say about the divorce?" asked Marty.

"Nothing," said Georgie. "She didn't tell us, so she doesn't want us to know."

"But we do know."

When Mrs. Thomas let them in, she gave them a hug. "You girls have been such good friends to Andrea," she said, "and that's so important to her right now."

"Is she OK?" asked Georgie.

"Why don't you go see for yourself?"

Andrea was propped up in bed with her left arm resting on a half dozen pillows. A portable television set had been moved into her room and she held the remote control in her right hand. When she saw Georgie and Marty, she aimed the remote at the set and jabbed the power button, turning off the picture in the middle of a Roadrunner cartoon.

"You got your own TV," observed Georgie.

"My dad sent it."

"Wish I had a TV in my room," said Marty.

"Maybe someday you'll break your arm," Georgie consoled her.

"I could break both arms, and I still wouldn't get a TV!"

"Yeah, my dad's great," said Andrea.

"Yeah, great," said Georgie. "Did he ever come to see you?" She didn't mean to say it. It just slipped out, and she was immediately sorry.

Andrea was defensive. "He's been busy. I told you he's real important."

"I know. I'm sorry."

"When he gets back from his trip he's going to take some time off and stay home with me every day till I can go back to school."

Georgie and Marty exchanged embarrassed glances.

"What's wrong?" asked Andrea. "Don't you believe me?"

"We know about the divorce," Georgie told her gently.

"Oh."

"It doesn't matter," said Marty.

"Yes, it does," said Andrea as tears slipped over her eyelids and rolled down her cheeks. "He wouldn't even come to see me in the hospital."

Georgie looked at Bruno standing watch by the window. "He was thinking about you," she told Andrea. "Look at the great stuff he sent."

"But he didn't come."

"Maybe he couldn't, you know, if it was an important trip."

"He wasn't on a trip," said Andrea bitterly. "He never takes trips."

"But you said . . ."

"I lied."

There was an awkward silence during which Andrea cried, and Georgie and Marty looked at their hands, at Bruno, at the ceiling—anywhere but at each other. Finally Georgie asked, "Do you want us to go?"

"No," said Andrea, wiping her face on the sleeve of her pajamas. "You know what he did?"

"Your dad?"

Andrea nodded. "He sent me a credit card to buy some school clothes."

"Wow," whispered Marty enviously.

"Yeah, but then he forgot," said Andrea. "He told them the card was stolen, and when I tried to use it . . ."

"They called security," said Georgie, remembering Andrea's pale, frightened face in the dress shop.

"I was so scared. I thought they were going to arrest me."

She wasn't shoplifting, thought Georgie.

"What happened?" asked Marty.

"They wouldn't believe me, so I had to call my mom."

"And that's how she found out you were at the mall," said Georgie.

"And grounded me for it," added Andrea.

Marty asked, "Why didn't you just call your dad?"

"I did, but he wouldn't talk to me."

"Why not?"

"He was in a meeting, or something. I said it was important, but I guess he didn't care."

"I don't think he did it on purpose," offered Georgie. "I mean, everybody forgets stuff."

"My mom forgot me one time," said Marty. "I was on a merry-go-round in front of the grocery store, and I looked up and saw her driving away."

"What happened?" asked Georgie.

"I just kept riding the merry-go-round until she came back."

"Weren't you scared?" asked Andrea.

"No. I knew she'd be back."

"My dad left Scott and me at school one time," said Andrea. "*I* sure was scared."

"He forgot to pick you up?" asked Georgie.

"Yeah. My mom came home and he was still at work. Boy, was she mad."

Marty grinned. "Did she yell at him?"

"They were always yelling at each other," said Andrea in a voice that matched the faraway look in her eyes. "I guess that's why they got a divorce."

Andrea stayed home for the rest of the week. Every afternoon Georgie and Marty visited her with the day's assignments from school. On Monday morning, the kids cheered when Andrea got on the bus. At school she was more popular than ever, but Georgie watched her classmates crowd around Andrea's table at lunch and she realized it didn't bother her anymore.

"Why does she keep doing that?" asked Marty.

"Doing what?"

"She keeps talking about her dad like he's something wonderful. How can she do that when he's so mean to her?"

"I don't think he's mean," said Georgie.

"Well, maybe not mean, but he's never around."

Something occurred to Georgie. "Maybe that's why Scott won't talk about him."

"See, that makes sense," said Marty, "but Andrea talks about him all the time."

Georgie shrugged. "She loves him."

"But, why?"

"He's her dad. Why does it bug you so much?"

Marty stuffed her napkin and straw into her

94

milk carton and smashed the top down. "I don't know," she said finally. "I think I don't believe her anymore. I bet her dad's not even a talent agent."

"I guess we'll find out next month."

"Why?"

"There's a concert at the civic center. Andrea said her dad's sending some tickets."

"You think he will?"

"Sure," said Georgie. "Why not?"

Georgie didn't know if Andrea's dad would send the concert tickets or not. Andrea had lied so many times, it was hard to decide when she was telling the truth. But Georgie had been wrong about the shoplifting, and so she was going to give Andrea the benefit of the doubt.

After lunch, Mr. Prescott announced that there would be a city-wide Science Fair and that he expected an entry from every student. Georgie got permission to work with Andrea and Marty on a single project, but they had no idea what they were going to do. When they sat together on the bus that afternoon, Georgie brought it up.

"We could draw a food web," said Andrea.

"You don't need three people to draw a food

web," said Georgie. "Besides Marty and I don't draw very well."

"Mr. Prescott said it could be anything."

"He also said if you're working together it has to be something really good," Georgie reminded her.

"Let's do an experiment," said Marty.

"What kind of experiment?" asked Georgie.

"I don't know."

"We could grow beans," said Andrea.

Georgie frowned. "What for?"

Andrea shrugged. "I just know they grow beans a lot in experiments."

Georgie giggled. "I think you're supposed to know why you're growing them, or it's not an experiment."

"It's gardening," agreed Marty and they all laughed.

What to do for the Science Fair occupied Georgie's mind for several days. Marty made suggestions now and then, but none of them seemed quite right to Georgie. Andrea was no help at all. On Saturday morning, Georgie awoke with an inspiration. She called Andrea and Marty and asked them to meet her at Mrs. Jenson's oak.

"Protective coloration," she told them when they had gathered at the tree. "That's what we'll do for the Science Fair."

"What about it?" asked Marty.

Andrea asked, "What is it?"

Georgie sighed. "It's like camouflage for animals."

"Like chameleons?"

"Yeah, but not just that," said Georgie. "There's a king snake that looks like a poisonous coral snake."

"Uh-uh. No snakes!" said Andrea shaking her head vigorously.

"That's just an example," said Georgie.

"I get it," said Marty. "If you think it's poisonous, you'll leave it alone."

Georgie nodded. "Right. So, what do you think?"

"About what?" asked Andrea.

"About doing our project on animals that protect themselves by pretending to be something else."

"Sounds great," said Marty, "but how do we do it?"

"I don't know yet," admitted Georgie. "Let's

start doing research and maybe we can think of something."

"Research?" Andrea's nose wrinkled up as she said the word.

Georgie laughed. "It won't kill you."

Georgie's mom took them to the library and helped them look for the books they needed. Georgie discovered insects that looked like sticks and leaves. Marty found butterflies with marks like giant eyes on their wings. Andrea complained that the books were too heavy for her to lift with her arm in a cast.

"If you're not going to help," Georgie told her, "you can just find your own project to do!"

"Georgie . . ." warned her mom.

Georgie's face felt hot. "Sorry," she mumbled, but she wasn't. It was how she felt. If Andrea wasn't going to contribute, Georgie didn't want her name on the project.

Georgie looked at Andrea. She was sitting with her head down cradling her cast in her right arm. Suddenly, Georgie really was sorry. She still meant what she said, but she was sorry she had lost her temper when she said it.

"It's OK," she told Andrea. "Marty and I can

look the stuff up and you can write it down for us."

Marty frowned at Georgie and went off to find some more books. Georgie's mom went to the card catalog. Georgie sat across from Andrea and tried to read, but every time she looked up she saw Andrea watching her through her bangs.

"I said I was sorry," Georgie told her.

"I know, but you act like you're still mad at me."

"I'm not mad," said Georgie. "I just think you should help us. It's cheating if you don't."

"I'll help," Andrea said eagerly. "Like you said, I'll write the stuff down."

Andrea made a show of opening her notebook and getting out her pencil to start on the notes. Georgie grinned. "OK. Let's make a list of all the animals we've found."

Georgie spread the books out on the table and Andrea started writing. After three words, she looked up. "Georgie?"

"Yeah?"

"Are you still going to the concert with me?"

"Sure, if your dad sends the tickets."

"He sent them. We got them yesterday."

"Great!" said Georgie, trying not to sound too surprised.

"But he only sent four—two for me and two for Scott."

"Oh. Then I guess you better take Marty."

"But I want you to go."

"You'll have more fun with Marty. She really likes concerts and stuff."

"I don't want to go with Marty," pouted Andrea.

"Why not? I thought you liked Marty." *Better than me*, thought Georgie, but didn't say it.

"She's OK," said Andrea, "but I like you best."

Georgie sat back in her chair with a heavy sigh, which caught in her throat as she glanced up. Marty was standing at the end of the table looking at them. There were tears in her eyes.

Chapter Nine

Georgie crawled into her father's lap and laid her head on his shoulder. He hugged her tightly and said, "What's wrong, Georgie Porgie?"

"Andrea made Marty cry."

"Your mom told me."

"Why does she like me best? I didn't even like her at all when I first met her."

"Maybe that's why."

Georgie sat up so she could see her dad's face.

"What's why?"

"Maybe she's just trying extra hard to get you to like her."

"Well, it didn't work," said Georgie. "I hate her now."

"I don't believe that."

"It's true. She . . ." Georgie didn't finish. Maybe he was right. Now that she had the chance to be rid of Andrea once and for all, Georgie discovered it wasn't what she wanted any more. "OK, but I'm still mad at her for hurting Marty's feelings."

"It's OK to be angry, Georgie, but you have to learn to hate the deed without hating the person."

Georgie put her head back down and snuggled her face into his neck. She could smell the Old Spice after-shave she had given him for Father's Day. "Stupid concert," she mumbled.

At Sunday school the next day her class talked about the moneychangers in the temple. Mrs. Denton said it showed that even Jesus got angry sometimes.

"My dad says you should hate the deed but not the person," said Georgie.

"I think your dad's exactly right," said Mrs. Denton.

"But what does he mean?"

"Well, let's see," Mrs. Denton began thoughtfully. "Anger is a powerful emotion, so you need to channel it in just the right way. How did Jesus channel His anger with the moneychangers?"

"He beat 'em up!" said Jonathan Mitchell.

Mrs. Denton laughed. "Not quite, Jonathan. He did run them out of the temple, but He directed His anger at what they were doing, not at them personally. Do you understand, Georgie?"

"I think so."

"Everything the Bible tells us about Jesus leads us to believe that He forgave the moneychangers, even though He was angry with them. And that's what He wants us to do."

"But what if someone just keeps on doing things that make you angry?" asked Georgie.

"'How many times shall I forgive my brother when he sins against me?'" Mrs. Denton quoted. "That's what Peter asked Jesus, and what did Jesus say?"

"Seventy-seven times."

Mrs. Denton nodded. "And what do you suppose He meant?"

"A whole bunch of times," said Georgie.

"That's right. He might just as well have said, 'How many times would you want to be forgiven, Peter?' And what would Peter have said?"

Nobody answered.

"Well," prompted Mrs. Denton, "how many times would *you* want to be forgiven, Georgie?"

Georgie grinned. "Every time."

Mrs. Denton winked at her. "Me, too."

The sun was bright and warm for October. After lunch the Grace Street Kids gathered on Georgie's front porch, all except Andrea.

"Where's Andrea?" asked Josh.

"She doesn't feel good," said Scott. "Mom even let her stay home from church this morning."

Georgie looked at Marty. "Maybe we should go see her."

"Not me," said Marty.

"Do you care if I go?"

"You can do what you want."

Georgie hesitated. "I'll just stay a few minutes," she said finally and walked down to Andrea's house.

Andrea was in her room watching TV. She didn't bother to turn the sound off when Georgie entered. "I thought you were mad at me," she said without looking up.

"I was," said Georgie.

"But you're not any more?"

"I got over it."

"I bet Marty's still mad at me."

"You hurt her feelings."

"I didn't mean to."

"I know."

"You think she'll stay mad at me forever?"

Georgie shrugged.

Tears stood in Andrea's eyes. "I can't help it if I like you best."

"Why does anybody have to like anybody best?" asked Georgie. "Why can't we just all be friends?"

"Because there's only two tickets," said Andrea.

Georgie sighed. "I gotta go."

"Do you have to?"

"I told Marty I'd be right back. We're going to work on the Science Fair project."

"Oh."

"See you tomorrow."

Georgie found Marty in her backyard sitting in a swing. She turned in one direction until the chains were tightly wound, then lifted her feet and let the swing spin back the other way.

She kept doing that—twist and spin, twist and spin—while Georgie stood and watched.

Finally, Georgie sat in the swing next to her and asked, "What're you doing?"

"Nothing."

"Andrea didn't mean what she said."

"It doesn't matter."

Georgie didn't say anything.

"I don't care what she says," insisted Marty.

"She's really sorry."

"I told you. I don't care."

Georgie thought a minute. "Are you ready to work on the Science Fair project?"

"I guess."

"I had an idea."

Marty stopped her swing and looked at Georgie. "What?"

"You know those hidden pictures?"

Marty nodded.

"What if we draw a great big picture with lots of animals hidden in it . . ."

"But you can't see them because they're camouflaged!" Marty finished for her.

"What do you think?"

"I think it's great. Let's do it."

They started by listing all the animals they could find that used camouflage for protection.

"The snake thing doesn't fit," observed Marty.

"Andrea will be happy about that."

"Do we still have to let Andrea help us?" Marty started walking toward her house.

"She can draw," Georgie reminded her as she followed. "We can't."

"Then let's do something else."

Georgie sighed. "Are you going to stay mad at Andrea forever?"

"I'm not mad."

"Yes, you are."

"I am not."

"Are too."

"Am not."

By then they were in Marty's room, sprawled

out on her bed. Georgie grabbed a fluffy, down pillow and tossed it into Marty's face. "OK, *Martha*, you win!"

Marty giggled and smacked the pillow across the top of Georgie's head. Georgie picked up another pillow and they launched into a full-scale battle.

"Martha Jane Wilson!"

Marty froze, her pillow suspended in midair.

"Do you girls know how much down pillows cost these days?" asked her mom from the bedroom door.

"Sorry," chorused Georgie and Marty.

Mrs. Wilson grinned. "Who was winning?"

Georgie and Marty laughed.

"Andrea's at the door," said Mrs. Wilson. "I asked her to come in, but she wouldn't."

Georgie looked at Marty.

"Don't look at me," said Marty. "She's your friend."

"She's *our* friend," said Georgie, grabbing Marty's wrist and dragging her to the front door.

"Hi," said Andrea through the screen.

"Why didn't you come in?" asked Georgie.

Andrea shrugged and looked at Marty.

Georgie gave Marty a little shove. Marty frowned, but said, "It's OK. Come on in."

Andrea stepped just inside the door. "Georgie said you're working on the Science Fair project."

"Yeah, so?"

"Well, I want to help, since it's my project, too."

"I thought you were sick."

"I'm better."

Marty didn't answer. She just turned and headed for her room. *At least Marty didn't say no,* thought Georgie as she and Andrea followed.

When they got to Marty's bedroom Andrea hesitated at the door. "I'm sorry I said that yesterday," she told Marty.

"It's OK," said Marty, pretending to be engrossed in her science book.

"Here." Andrea pulled two concert tickets from her pocket and handed them to Georgie.

"I—I can't go," said Georgie.

"You mean you won't go," Andrea corrected her, "because Marty can't go. And Marty wouldn't go with me now if I begged her. So, there are the tickets. You and Marty can have them."

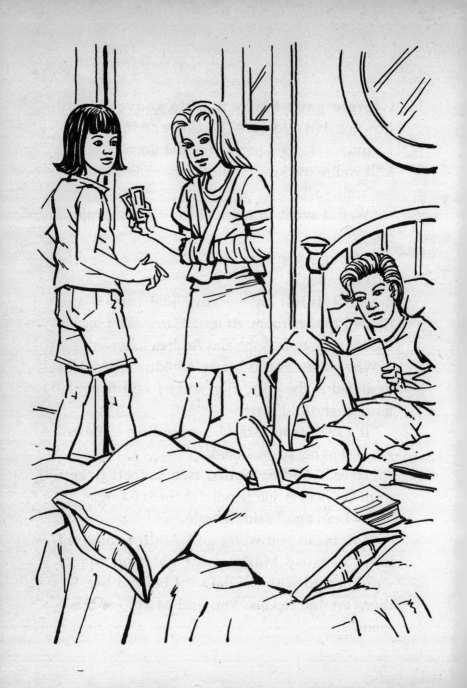

"But what about you?" asked Georgie.

"I can go next time. It's no big deal."

Georgie stared at the tickets. Marty stared at Andrea. Andrea said, "Maybe I'd better go home."

"Oh, no, you don't!" said Marty. "You've got to help us with this science project."

"You mean it?"

"Well, we're not going to do all the work and then let you take part of the credit. Are we Georgie?"

Georgie grinned. "No way!"

Chapter Ten

On the day the Science Fair projects were due, Marty's mom took them to school. Andrea had drawn a giant jungle scene that would have been impossible to carry on the bus. It barely fit into the trunk of Mrs. Wilson's car. Georgie fumed and fussed until the trunk lid clicked shut.

"It will be just fine back there," Mrs. Wilson assured her. "You girls have done a wonderful job."

Georgie had painted the scene with water-colors, mixing blues and yellows to make dozens of different shades of green. Marty wrote descriptions of the animals, explaining their use of protective coloration. The she had put the descriptions with a diagram showing where each animal was hidden in the picture.

Georgie could hardly wait to get to school. When they carried the project down the hall to Mr. Prescott's room—it took all three of them—kids kept stopping them to look at the picture. Mr. Prescott smiled broadly and helped them set it up at the front of the classroom. Georgie was sure they would win a ribbon, maybe even the blue one.

At lunch, when the kids crowded around Andrea, they had something to talk about besides her father.

"It was Georgie's idea," she told them.

"But Andrea drew the picture," said Georgie.

"Georgie painted it," countered Andrea, "and Marty did most of the research."

"And all of the writing," added Georgie.

"We did it together," said Marty.

"Like the Three Musketeers!" said Georgie.

"O-o-o, I want a candy bar!" said Andrea.

That afternoon, when Mr. Prescott asked for volunteers to present their projects, Georgie raised her hand, stretching her arm as high as she could and waving it from side to side. Mr. Prescott noticed and let them go first.

After the presentation, Andrea whispered, "You think they liked it?"

"They asked a bunch of questions," said Georgie.

"Is that good or bad?" asked Marty.

Georgie shrugged. "Mostly they were smiling."

"Including Mr. Prescott," said Marty, "and that's all I care about!"

"Yeah," agreed Andrea. "If we win a ribbon he'll have to give us A's."

Georgie felt sure they'd win a ribbon. She wasn't as sure that Mr. Prescott would have to give them A's for it, but she didn't say so.

"Then we'll get to be in the school Science Fair," she said, "and if we win that . . ."

"We go to the local, and then citywide," Marty finished for her.

"What if we win that?" asked Andrea.

Marty looked at Georgie. Georgie shrugged. "Guess we'll find out."

"*If* we win," Marty reminded her.

In the morning, they raced off the school bus and down the hall, moving as fast as they could without getting yelled at for running in the halls. At Mr. Prescott's door, Georgie stopped suddenly and the others skidded into her. Taped to the corner of their project was a bright yellow ribbon.

"What does yellow mean?" asked Andrea.

"I don't know," said Georgie, looking around the room. "All the ribbons are yellow."

"It means you've been selected," said Mr. Prescott, walking up behind them.

"You mean we won?" asked Georgie.

"If you want to look at it that way. These entries from each class were selected to represent the fifth grade in the Science Fair. Yours was one of them."

"But, I thought . . ." began Andrea, but didn't finish.

"You thought there'd be red, white, and blue ribbons," guessed Mr. Prescott, "and there will be, just not yet."

"Oh."

Mr. Prescott laughed. "Cheer up, girls. You've done a lot of hard work and made a science project you can be proud of. Now go to your classes. You're going to be late."

On Friday morning, all the selected projects from each grade level were set up on the gymnasium for the Science Fair. Students were allowed to visit the Fair during their regular science period. When it was their class's turn, Georgie, Marty, and Andrea marched solemnly down the hall. The projects had already been judged, and so they would know immediately if their picture had won. Georgie's stomach felt hollow and full at the same time, and sort of fluttery.

"Well, even if we didn't get a ribbon," she said, "we know we did our best, and that's what's important."

"Yeah," Andrea agreed. "At least we got to be in the Fair."

"Right," said Marty, "and we've still got our A's."

"*Please,* let us have a ribbon!" begged Georgie.

When they found the fifth-grade aisle, Georgie stopped and turned her back to it. "You look," she told them. "I can't."

She squeezed her eyes shut and crossed all the fingers on both hands. When she heard Marty squeal, Georgie's eyes flew open and she spun around. Halfway down the aisle Andrea and Marty were jumping up and down in a little, circular dance. Georgie ran to them. A large, blue ribbon had joined the yellow one in the corner of their picture.

"Winning isn't everything," her father reminded her over the pot roast and mashed potatoes at dinner that night.

"I know," said Georgie.

"But it sure does feel good," he added with a wink.

Georgie grinned. "And first place feels even better."

"We're very proud of you," said her mom, "not because you won, but because you did such a good job on your project."

"Not just me," said Georgie. "Marty and Andrea, too."

"I know, and you were afraid Andrea wouldn't do her part."

"Yeah."

"Is everything all patched up between her and Marty?" asked Georgie's dad.

Georgie nodded. "She gave the concert tickets to Marty and me."

"Then she's not going?"

"No. Just us and Scott and Michael."

"But her mom's still going."

"She's going to take us, but there are only four tickets," said Georgie.

Her dad sighed. "I'm sorry, Georgie, but you and Michael are just too young to go to a concert without an adult."

Georgie looked at Michael who shrugged. "We'll go tell them after dinner."

Mrs. Thomas answered the door. "We can't go," said Georgie, holding out the tickets.

"Why not, Georgie? Andrea really wants you to have them."

"I know, but . . ."

"Our dad won't let us go without an adult," said Michael.

"Oh, I see. Well, come on in," said Mrs. Thomas, "while I make a phone call. Maybe we can work something out."

After she went into the kitchen, Michael shook his head. "Dad's not going to change his mind."

"About what?" asked Andrea, coming in from the hallway.

"We can't go to the concert," Georgie told her.

"Stupid concert," said Andrea.

Georgie's eyes opened wide in surprise.

Andrea grinned. "If my stupid dad hadn't sent those stupid tickets to that stupid concert . . ." She broke off into giggles.

"We wouldn't have had that stupid fight," Georgie finished, and they both laughed.

Mrs. Thomas bustled back into the living room. "It's all settled. Mr. Thomas is going to get us two more tickets. They won't be with the others, but you and Scott won't mind sitting by yourselves, will you Michael?"

Michael grinned and shook his head. Georgie said, "*Two* tickets?"

Mrs. Thomas nodded. "One for me and one for Andrea."

The concert was on a Friday night. That afternoon Mrs. Thomas picked the kids up right after school. They had to go by Mr. Thomas' office for the extra tickets.

"My dad's going to take us all out to dinner," said Andrea.

"If he isn't too busy," warned her mom.

"He won't be. He promised."

"He doesn't always know when he's going to be busy, Andrea."

Georgie sneaked a look at Marty. Marty made a face and Georgie looked away to keep from laughing. Andrea turned around suspiciously.

"What's going on?"

"Nothing," said Georgie.

Marty came to her rescue. "We were just wondering if there will be any famous people at your dad's office."

Andrea grinned. "Maybe."

"Maybe not," said Scott.

The agency where Mr. Thomas worked was on the fourteenth floor of a high-rise in the middle of the city. When the elevator doors opened, they stepped into a large waiting area. A receptionist sat behind a circular desk surrounded by red leather sofas and chairs. Georgie looked at every face in the room but didn't recognize anyone.

"Good evening, Mrs. Thomas," said the receptionist. A sign on the desk said her name was Carol White.

Mrs. Thomas said, "Good evening, Carol. Would you tell Mr. Thomas we're here?"

"I'm afraid he's out with a client," said Carol, holding out an envelope, "but he left these for you."

"He was going to take us to dinner," complained Andrea.

Scott said, "Shut up, Andrea."

Andrea was quiet all through dinner at Georgie's favorite hamburger place. When they got to the concert, she cheered up a little, but not much. Georgie had fun, but she was glad when it was all over and Mrs. Thomas let her and Michael out at the end of their driveway.

"I guess Andrea's dad really is a big shot," she said.

"I guess so," agreed Michael.

"It was hard to tell, the way she pretends about him all the time."

"Yeah. Scott does, too, only he pretends that he doesn't even have a dad."

"Well, he doesn't," said Georgie. "Not really."

Michael paused with his hand on the door-knob and looked thoughtfully at Georgie. "I guess you're right."

The city-wide Science Fair was held on Saturday at the civic center's exhibition hall, with more than a dozen school systems participating in the competition. Georgie strolled up and down the aisles with her dad looking at home-made light bulbs and algae experiments. They made the hidden picture project seem kind of silly to her.

"Maybe we had a dumb idea," she said.

Her dad squeezed her hand. "Don't be silly, Georgie Porgie. If your project wasn't good, you wouldn't be here."

"I guess, but I bet we don't win anything."

"I bet if you'd stop worrying about it, you might actually have a good time!"

Georgie grinned. It felt so good to have her dad there. Marty's dad had come, too, but Andrea was still planted by the door waiting for hers to show up.

At noon, Georgie's family met the Wilsons and the Thomases for lunch. Georgie couldn't eat

knowing, at that very moment, the judges were making their decisions about the projects. She squirmed and picked at her sandwich until her mother finally gave her permission to leave the table. Andrea and Marty quit their lunches in mid-bite to go with her.

"There it is," said Georgie breathlessly, rounding the corner of the fifth-grade section.

"I think there's a ribbon on it," said Marty.

There was—a green one with the words HONORABLE MENTION stamped in gold letters. Georgie stared at it. "I guess it's better than nothing." she said finally.

"Is this your project?" asked a tall man with glasses and thick, gray hair. On the pocket of his suit coat was a gold ribbon that said he was a Science Fair judge.

"Yes, it's ours," Georgie managed.

"Well, I think it's very creative," he told her and handed her a business card. "I'm a publisher, and I'd like to talk to you a little later about using a picture of you and your project as an illustration in one of our science textbooks."

Georgie tried to swallow. "Sure."

The man smiled. "When I've finished judging,

I'll meet you back here," he said, and walked off down the aisle.

Suddenly they were surrounded by moms and dads and brothers and sisters all hugging them at the same time. It was better than winning first prize. Georgie grinned at Marty and looked for Andrea, but Andrea was gone.

"We'll be right back," Georgie told her mom, then grabbed Marty's hand and said, "Come on."

They found Andrea sitting on the floor with her back against the wall just outside the doors of the exhibition hall. Georgie and Marty sat down, one on each side of her.

"I hate him," said Andrea.

"Your dad?" asked Georgie.

Andrea nodded. "I can see his building right through that window. He could have come, if he had wanted to."

Georgie and Marty exchanged helpless glances.

"I hate him," repeated Andrea.

"No, you don't," said Georgie. "You love him."

"Well, he doesn't love me."

"Yes he does."

"He doesn't act like it."

"That's because he's stupid," said Georgie.

Andrea looked up and smiled.

"Who needs him, anyway?" asked Marty. "we've got one another!"

"Like the Three Musketeers," said Georgie.

"O-o-o, let's go get a candy bar," said Andrea.